WELCOME TO

Beast Quest

Collect the special coins in th
You will earn one gold coin fo
every chapter you read.

Once you have finished all the chapters,
find out what to do with your gold coins at
the back of the book.

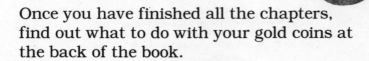

With special thanks to Conrad Mason

www.beastquest.co.uk

ORCHARD BOOKS

First published in Great Britain in 2017 by The Watts Publishing Group

1 3 5 7 9 10 8 6 4 2

Text © 2017 Beast Quest Limited.
Cover and inside illustrations by Steve Sims
© Beast Quest Limited 2017

Beast Quest is a registered trademark of Beast Quest Limited
Series created by Beast Quest Limited, London

A CIP catalogue record for this book is available from the British Library.

ISBN 978 1 40834 301 2

Printed in Great Britain

The paper and board used in this book are made from wood from responsible sources

Orchard Books
An imprint of Hachette Children's Group
Part of The Watts Publishing Group Limited
Carmelite House, 50 Victoria Embankment, London EC4Y 0DZ

An Hachette UK Company
www.hachette.co.uk
www.hachettechildrens.co.uk

MAGROR
OGRE OF THE SWAMPS

BY ADAM BLADE

ORCHARD

CONTENTS

STORY ONE

THREE HEROES

The smell of the ogre was in his nostrils now, a sickening stink of swamp water. Taladon tried to roll away, but the Beast stamped on his shoulder, crushing him into the mud.

The ogre loomed above, a four-armed bulk of shadow. He raised a fist as big as a boulder, blotting out the blood-red sun of Gorgonia. Any second now, it would come slamming down to break Taladon's skull like an egg. Then down it came, speeding faster and—

"There you are, Tom! I've been looking for you everywhere!"

Tom looked up from his desk, startled out of the story by Elenna's voice.

His friend stood framed in the ancient stone doorway, hands planted on her hips. It was dark in the library, but Tom could see her face in the warm glow of his reading candle. She was grinning. "Everyone else is in bed," she said. "And here you are hunched over a dusty old book!"

Tom smiled back at her. "Not just any book, Elenna." He brushed his fingers across the faded yellow pages. "It's the *Chronicles of Avantia*."

"That's a strange choice for a bedtime story," said Elenna. She came to perch on the desk beside him, weaving between worn leather books piled up on the floor.

"Actually, I'm reading about my father," said Tom. "Something that happened to him a long time ago, when he wasn't much older than I am now."

"Let's hear it, then! If it's a story about your father, I bet it's a good one."

Tom smiled. Elenna was right – the tale of Magror the Swamp Ogre was just as thrilling and adventurous as he had hoped. "Are you ready?" he asked, turning back to the start of the story. The candle flickered, sending shadows creeping across the page like living creatures.

Then with a deep breath, Tom began to read.

A KING ON THE RUN

"Let the duel begin!" cried King Theo, bringing his arm down in a sweeping stroke as he sat forward on his throne.

Taladon watched closely as the two men standing before the king bowed, then stepped apart, circling each other. Each held a rapier, the long, slender blades glinting in the morning sunshine that filtered through the palace windows.

The courtiers had cleared a wide space in the centre of the throne room for the show of swordplay. Taladon didn't expect it to last long. He had never heard of Tristan Harkman – a young soldier with a mop of brown hair – before today. But Tristan's opponent was famous throughout Avantia – Sir Lennard, a nobleman from the north, and victor of the Great Tournament. *And as of this morning, our new Master of the Beasts!*

Lennard pretended to lunge forward, and laughed as Harkman darted away. He was a head taller than Harkman, with a jutting jaw, a mane of thick blond hair poking out from beneath his helmet, and a waxed moustache.

The rest of him was covered in the glittering Golden Armour of a Master of the Beasts. Taladon couldn't take his eyes off the fabled armour. No one had worn it in a very long time – not since a former Mistress of the Beasts had set off on a Quest and never returned.

Lennard spun on his heel, rapier whirling, pausing to smile and wink at a group of court ladies who blushed deeply. "The art of swordplay is in the dance," he pronounced. "No commoner can ever truly master it. Their feet are too lumpen! Too clumsy!"

As if to prove it, Lennard dodged to one side and slapped Harkman on the cheek with the side of his sword, the sound ringing through the throne room.

Titters rose from among the courtiers, but Harkman just grunted and gritted his teeth.

Taladon looked sideways at the royal party. He couldn't be certain, but he thought he saw King Theo frown slightly.

Sitting at the King's side was Queen Rosalind, resplendent in green velvet. Next to her stood her sons, the Crown Prince Angelo and Prince Hugo. *And me!* thought Taladon. It still felt strange to be here with Avantia's most powerful family. *But I'm only Prince Hugo's squire.*

Harkman charged forwards, swinging his rapier. But Lennard simply skipped out of range, leaving Harkman to stumble across the polished stone floor. The laughter of the courtiers grew louder, and Lennard flashed a grin all around the throne room.

Taladon felt his jaw clench. *I'd*

love to wipe that smile off his face!
Lennard was a talented swordsman,
but there was no need to humiliate
Harkman just to prove it. Lennard
had the advantage of the Golden
Armour too, which was said to
enhance its wearer's swordfighting
skills, as well as giving them great
strength, speed and courage.

Harkman whirled round with a face
like thunder. "I'd like to see you try
that on a battlefield," he muttered.

Lennard tutted. "A true warrior can
face his foe under any circumstances,
young man. Now, have you tired
yourself out yet?"

Harkman's face went red with
anger, and he charged again. This
time Lennard ducked down low,

swinging his leg round and tripping the young soldier. Harkman fell heavily on the flagstones and his rapier skittered away.

As the courtiers roared with laughter, Lennard pretended to yawn. "Is this really the best man King Theo's army has to offer?"

Before he knew what he was doing, Taladon had stepped forward. "I'll fight you," he said.

Silence fell over the throne room, and Taladon felt heat rush into his face. *What am I doing?*

"You?" said Lennard, his lip curling. "A simple squire?"

Taladon felt a hand on his arm, and looked up into Prince Hugo's face. "Lennard is a talented swordsman," said the prince. "You don't have to do this." He lowered his voice so that only Taladon could hear. "But if you do…make sure you give him a smack for me."

"Let's get it over with," said Lennard. He kicked Harkman's sword across the floor to rest at Taladon's feet.

Taladon shook his head. "We'll fight with spears."

"This puppy knows nothing," said Lennard, with a sigh. "Spears! What sort of duel—"

"I thought a true warrior could face his foe under any circumstances," interrupted Taladon.

Lennard scowled and looked up at the throne. A smile twitched at the corners of King Theo's mouth. Then he gave a nod.

"Very well," snarled Lennard, as two soldiers stepped forward with spears. "At least this will be quick!"

Taladon took his weapon, feeling the weight. He swung it in a figure of eight, hearing it sing through the air. A murmur spread through the court.

I practise every day... Let's hope it pays off!

He stepped out to face Lennard.

"Begin!" called King Theo.

Lennard leapt forward at once, stabbing with his spear. Taladon knocked the blow aside with his spear shaft and brought the butt round. It clanged against Lennard's shoulder armour, sending him staggering to the side.

Lennard rallied, swiping low with
his spear, but Taladon jumped over
the shaft and struck again, shoving
the butt of his own spear into

Lennard's breastplate and forcing him further back.

The Master of the Beasts glared at Taladon, eyes wide with fury. Something wasn't right, though. *The Golden Armour is supposed to give its wearer incredible strength...and speed, too!* For some reason, it didn't seem like it was working.

Taladon stepped closer, hefting his spear. *Lennard's nimble, but he's arrogant. If I can find an opening, this should be over in—*

There was a sudden *BANG* and a flash of light. Taladon dropped his spear and stumbled away, blinking. Gasps and cries rose up all around the chamber.

Taladon blinked away the spots

dancing across his vision, and saw that Lennard looked just as shocked as he was. In between them, a magical doorway had taken shape in mid-air, its edges wreathed in crackling blue light. Then someone stepped out of it and fell to their knees.

Taladon rushed to help the stranger up. It was a frail old man, dressed in red robes that were tattered and torn. He was wearing a silver crown.

"King Arun!" said King Theo, on his feet now. All eyes locked on to the new arrival. *The King of Gorgonia*, Taladon realised. *But what's he doing here?*

King Arun tore free and stumbled towards the throne. He was panting heavily, and his eyes were wild

and staring. "Help me!" he gasped.
"Please... They're coming after me!"

"Slow down..." said Prince Angelo,
stepping forward with a hand
outstretched. "Who's after you?"

A sound rose from within the portal
– a clattering of beating wings. And
rising above it came squalling cries
that chilled Taladon's blood.

King Theo gestured to his guards.
"Find the wizard Aduro," he ordered.
"We have to close the portal,
before—"

Too late. A flock of creatures burst
from the doorway, whirling into the
throne room in a black tide.

Leathery wings fluttered on all
sides, and for a moment Taladon
thought the creatures were bats.

But they were far bigger, each wing
stretching out longer than the height
of a man. Their long jaws hinged and
clicked ferociously, each loaded with
rows of deadly, needle-like teeth.

Karr-aaak! Karr-aaak! Karr-aaak!

With a bloodcurdling squeal the
first of the creatures swooped down
towards King Arun, like a vulture on
to a carcass...

1

QUEST TO GORGONIA

"I'll save him!" shouted Sir Lennard, rushing towards King Arun. But another bat-like creature whipped past, striking the Master of the Beasts hard on the head. His helmet spun around, and Lennard tripped, clattering on to the ground with a sound like a great avalanche of pots and pans.

The first monster had almost reached King Arun, and stretched out its hooked claws towards his neck...

Taladon snatched up his spear and hurled it as hard as he could, barely stopping to take aim.

The spear struck the creature squarely. *Whoosh!* Instead of falling dead, it burst apart in an explosion of green light. When Taladon looked again, there wasn't a trace of it left.

It's not a real animal at all! It's conjured out of pure magic.

The throne room rang with the screams of courtiers, and the savage cries of the swooping monsters. Taladon whirled round and saw one of the bat creatures diving towards him, its jaws gaping wide, needle-like teeth glinting horribly. Taladon raised his spear, but he knew it wouldn't be fast enough to stop the monster.

Whoosh! The huge magical bat exploded with light, leaving green spots in Taladon's vision. An arrow clattered to the floor beside him,

fallen from the body of the destroyed monster.

"Lucky I was here to save you, farm boy," said a familiar voice. Taladon saw Harkman with a bow in his hand, the string still humming. Taladon opened his mouth to thank his rescuer, but Harkman was glowering. "This is no place for you. Leave the fighting to the real soldiers."

Before Taladon could reply, Harkman fitted another arrow to his bow and took aim at a flock of four bat creatures swooping towards King Theo. Angelo and Hugo had drawn their swords and formed a shield around their father. They swiped at the creatures with their blades, but Angelo cried out and fell to his knees as one raked his back with its talons. The next moment it exploded in a flash of green light, struck by a curved knife thrown by Queen Rosalind.

Wheeling, the creatures all turned from the Avantian royal family and descended on King Arun.

This is no place for you... Taladon replayed the words in his mind, and felt a surge of determination. *We'll see about that!* Racing across the throne room, Taladon grabbed his spear from where it had fallen beside the cowering King Arun. Looking up, he saw that Harkman had arrived too.

"Didn't you hear me?" said Harkman. "I said—" Then the

creatures came shrieking down on them.

Standing guard over King Arun, Taladon cut and thrust with his spear, while Harkman launched arrow after arrow through the air. One by one, the bat-like monsters exploded with green flashes. Taladon counted them off quickly. *Still one to go... But where is it?*

Suddenly he was grabbed from behind, his cloak straining at his neck as he was lifted into the air. Taladon looked up and saw the final creature flapping higher, clutching the end of his cloak in its talons.

He writhed, trying to stab at the creature with his spear, but it swung him out of reach. *Only one thing for it*... Swinging his spear round, he sliced behind his head, ripping his cloak so that he fell towards the floor.

He tucked himself into a forward roll as he landed, coming up a short distance away. From behind, he heard the howl of the creature as it dived down towards him. He thrust backwards with his spear,

heard a *BANG* and saw the flash of green reflected on the flagstones as it exploded.

Everything was quiet in the throne room, except for the panting of the fighters. Then there came the shuffle of courtiers' feet, as they emerged from behind tapestries, tables and chairs. Then someone began to clap.

"Impressive... Very impressive."

Taladon turned at the voice. A blue-robed man with a dark beard and thick dark hair had entered the throne room. Taladon's heart beat a little faster. He had seen this man perform magical spells that Taladon could hardly believe, even though he saw them with his own eyes. Taladon bowed his head.

"Thank you, Wizard Aduro," he mumbled.

Aduro nodded. Casually, he raised his hand and curled it into a fist. At once, the crackling blue doorway collapsed in on itself, leaving nothing but a few blue sparks that soon died away.

"Phew!" said Lennard. "We soon saw them off, didn't we?" The Master of the Beasts rose up from behind a heavy oak chest, straightening his helmet.

"I trust you were comfortable down there?" said Aduro, raising an eyebrow at the nobleman.

"I was forming a rear-guard," mumbled Lennard. "In case one of those horrors tried to escape."

"Didn't see him take out a single one," said Harkman, in a low voice. Taladon grinned and tried to catch the soldier's eye, but Harkman just scowled and looked away.

"Forgive me, please," said King Arun, as he rose and dusted off his robes. "It was I who brought those monsters to Avantia."

"But where do they come from?" asked Prince Hugo.

King Arun's face darkened. "I'm afraid they are servants of Malvel, the Dark Wizard. He has invaded Gorgonia and taken my castle."

Taladon felt a cold weight settle in his stomach at the mention of Malvel. The Dark Wizard had been banished from Avantia only a season before.

And now he's back...

"If what King Arun says is true, then this isn't over, Your Highness," said Aduro, bowing to King Theo. "Malvel is a deadly opponent. And once he has Gorgonia in his grasp, he will turn to Avantia."

King Theo nodded. "My thoughts exactly. We must send a warrior to Gorgonia to face the Dark Wizard and regain the kingdom for our friend, King Arun." He turned to Sir Lennard. "Master of the Beasts. You are our champion. Are you ready to face Malvel and defeat him?"

Lennard swallowed, and his eyes went wide. "Of course I am," he huffed. "But surely I should stay here, at my king's side? What's the sense

in rushing off to Gorgonia, when
Avantia needs my protection?"

"Perhaps this task is not entirely...
suitable for our Master of the Beasts,"
said Aduro. "But who will go, if not
Sir Lennard?"

Taladon felt something rising up

inside him – a warm glow of courage.
Somehow he knew that he would do
whatever it took to protect Avantia,
and Gorgonia too. "Let me go," he
said, before he could think it through.
"I will defeat the Dark Wizard!"

THROUGH THE PORTAL

Everyone stared at Taladon again.

"You?" spat Harkman. "Forgive me,
Your Majesty, but I beg you to send
me instead. This squire might know
a few tricks with his spear, but he has
no *real* experience. He's never even
seen a battle."

Taladon cast a glance at the soldier,
but once again, Harkman wouldn't

meet his eye. *Why does he dislike me so?*

Murmurs swelled throughout the courtroom, until King Theo raised a hand for silence. "You are a brave young man, Harkman," he said, thoughtfully. "But so is Taladon. We all saw his prowess against Malvel's creatures just now. And my son, Prince Hugo, speaks most highly of him."

Taladon felt himself blushing at the king's praise.

"However," the king continued, "Malvel will be a far greater opponent than those creatures of magic. And for this reason, I will send all three of you."

Taladon gulped. *All three of us?*

"Sire—" began Lennard.

"It is decided," interrupted King Theo. "Sir Lennard, young Harkman and Taladon the Squire – I charge you to travel to Gorgonia, and return only once our enemy is brought to justice!"

Applause thundered on all sides. Only Taladon, Lennard and Harkman were silent. Looking at his companions, Taladon could have sworn that they had both turned pale. He thought of the Dark Wizard, and felt a chill run down his own spine too. *What have I done?* But it was too late for second thoughts.

"Thank you, brave warriors," said King Arun. "Gorgonia is eternally grateful. May you return victorious – and soon!"

Aduro the wizard took a step forward, and with a quick flick of his wrist a curved horn took shape in mid-air, glittering gold and carved with swirling patterns. Aduro placed the horn in Lennard's hands.

"This horn is magical," said Aduro. "It sounds across the worlds. If you blow it in Gorgonia I will hear its call in Avantia. Once your Quest is

completed, sound this horn, and I shall create a portal for you to return."

"And if we...er...fail in our Quest?" said Lennard, his voice trembling.

Aduro didn't seem to hear him. "You may leave at once," said the wizard. He muttered a spell under his breath, and with a thunderous cracking sound, another portal opened in the middle of the room. This one was a shimmering white tunnel, so bright it hurt to look at. Courtiers gasped and cowered away, but Taladon felt a fresh energy stirring through his body. *Time for the Quest to begin...*

"This portal will take you close to the Gorgonian castle," said Aduro. "Good luck, and I hope we shall see all three of you return very soon."

"Hope?" said Lennard.

Taladon took a step towards the shimmering portal, but Harkman cut in front of him. "Best I go first, farm boy," said the soldier. "There might be danger ahead."

"If there is, I'll be ready for it," Taladon shot back, but Harkman had already turned and leapt into the white tunnel. In a flash he was gone.

Taladon paused to bow to King Theo, then to King Arun. Grasping his spear, he followed Harkman, plunging into the heart of the portal.

For an instant, Taladon felt as though he were falling, faster and faster, rushing winds buffeting him. White light filled his vision, and his mouth fell open in a silent scream. Then with a shocking jolt, he was standing still.

Taladon felt dizzy. The throne room was gone. Around him, the ground stretched out on all sides, carpeted with long grey grasses that swayed in a gentle breeze. The sky was dark, tinged with red as though at sunset. There was silence, except for the rustling of the grass. *We're not in Avantia any more.*

A clatter and a thump behind him broke the peace, and he turned to see Sir Lennard picking himself up from the grass, dusting off Aduro's golden horn. Behind him, the white portal blinked away into nothingness.

"Which way do we go?" Taladon

wondered out loud.

"Isn't it obvious?" said Harkman's voice. Taladon turned and saw the soldier a short distance away, pointing to the horizon. A black fortress stood there, bold against the sky. A line of thick, dark jungle lay in front of it.

"Completely obvious, of course," said Lennard. "Follow me, you two. And don't be afraid. You have a Master of the Beasts with you!"

"How many Beasts have you actually defeated?" asked Taladon.

Lennard went purple. "What an absurd question! It's not about the number I've—"

"How many have you seen, then?" asked Harkman.

"Oh, hundreds!" said Lennard,

brightening. "My father has an entire hall full of paintings."

"So we'll be fine," muttered Taladon. "As long as Malvel's Beasts are just pictures."

For once, Harkman's mouth

flickered into a brief, grim smile.

They set off, wading through the grey grass towards the distant castle. The ground rose and fell in gentle waves, and as they reached the top of a slope, they saw a cluster of thatched houses built around a stone well, beyond. *A village!*

Lennard dropped into a crouch.

"What's wrong?" said Harkman.

"Gorgonians!" whispered Lennard. "Down there! They might eat us."

Harkman spluttered with laughter. "Gorgonians don't eat people, take it from me."

"How do you know?" hissed Lennard.

"Well, I don't know for certain," Harkman admitted.

"I'm sure they're ordinary people, just like Avantians," said Taladon. "I'm going to ask them the quickest way to the castle."

"Not without me, you're not," said Harkman.

"Wait!" squealed Sir Lennard, but Taladon was already striding down the slope, with Harkman following.

"Lennard might have a point," said Harkman. "We don't know how friendly they'll be to strangers."

I'm sure they'll be friendlier than you, thought Taladon, but he bit his lip. "It'll be fine," he replied instead. "Just trust—"

Then the ground gave way beneath his feet, and they both plummeted down into darkness.

INTERROGATION

THUMP!

Taladon's body jolted as he hit the ground. He groaned and rolled over, his left side throbbing with pain. Harkman lay beside him, muttering curses as he pushed himself up on to his elbows.

They were in a circular pit, dug into the dark Gorgonian soil. The hole was three times the height of a man and a

couple of paces wide. *A hunting pit.* It
had to be. They were lucky it wasn't
lined with spikes.

"I told you so!" snapped a voice
from above. Clambering to his feet,
Taladon saw Lennard leaning over
the edge of the pit. "They catch people
in these traps, then eat them!"

"I'm sure this pit is just for wild
animals," said Harkman, but he didn't
sound very confident. "Get us out of
here, will you?"

Suddenly Lennard's head jerked up,
and he froze.

"What's wrong?" Taladon
demanded.

"Villagers!" hissed Lennard.
"They're coming up the hillside.
They've got torches! And scythes, and

pitchforks. And...they look rather angry."

"Then hurry up!" growled Harkman.

"Look here," said Lennard. "There's no sense in us all getting captured. I'm going to hide. Don't worry, I'll watch and see if they're hostile. If so, I'll save you, mark my words."

"Don't you dare!" shouted Harkman, but Lennard had already disappeared from view, and Taladon heard the nobleman's footsteps as he ran away up the slope.

"Good to know our Master of the Beasts is looking out for us," said Taladon, rolling his eyes.

Harkman just shook his head angrily, then beat a fist against the dirt wall of the pit.

Moments later, Taladon saw the glow of torches above them. The faces of the villagers appeared at the edge of the pit, glaring down at them. *They look just like Avantians. Furious ones...*

"Let me explain," Taladon called up to them. "We're here to help!"

"Rubbish!" snarled a villager with a long, plaited red beard. "You're Avantians. Don't try to deny it! We saw the portal open in the sky."

"Where are our children?" roared a young woman who was trembling with rage. "*He* stole them – your evil wizard! What have you done with them?"

Malvel, thought Taladon. "Let us explain," he said. "Malvel's an Avantian like us, but we're trying to stop him."

"A likely story," scoffed the red-bearded villager. "You're coming with us, the pair of you, and if we don't like what you have to say, it'll be the end of you both!"

A rancid tomato hit Taladon with a wet *smack*, and slid down his face. He blinked and spat out pulp.

His neck and wrists were locked into wooden stocks. If he strained his neck, he could see Harkman to his left, just as trapped as he was. The villagers stood a few feet away, hurling rotten fruit and vegetables from wooden crates and sacks they had brought along to the village square.

"Take that!" shrieked an old man, hurling a turnip over Taladon's head.

"To be honest, I was expecting worse," murmured Taladon.

"Wait till one of the cabbages hits you," said Harkman. "They're harder than you'd think."

Taladon grinned. That was one good thing about being trapped in the stocks. *Harkman has no choice but to*

talk to me now!

"And here's our saviour," said Harkman, bitterly. "This gets better and better." He nodded his head a little. Taladon scanned the crowd and saw a tall man hovering at the back of the village square, dressed in a thick hooded cloak, with gold armour glinting underneath.

It's me, mouthed Lennard, from under the hood. He gave them a thumbs up, then dodged behind a cart as a frail old woman cast a glance at him.

"What a coward!" growled Harkman. "He's a fine swordsman, I'll give him that. But what use is skill if you have no courage?"

A carrot struck the wooden stocks beside him with a hollow *thunk*.

"That's what I don't understand," said Taladon, frowning. "Lennard's wearing the Golden Armour, isn't he? And I thought the chainmail was supposed to give its wearer magical bravery."

Harkman snorted. "Then he's an

even bigger coward than I thought!"

Or the armour isn't working...

Taladon sighed. "If only we had a real Master of the Beasts."

"One who's actually faced a Beast before," agreed Harkman.

Out of the corner of his eye, Taladon saw Harkman smiling, and smiled back. Then he noticed someone approaching, and the smile froze.

It was a huge man, built like a bull, with a flattened nose and a long silver ponytail running down his back. He had stripped to the waist, and was tugging something from his belt – a vicious-looking black leather horse whip. "Enough of the games," the giant man shouted at the other villagers. "I'll whip some sense into these Avantians!" He cracked his whip, so loudly that several bystanders flinched away. "Where are they?" he snarled at Taladon. "Where are our children?"

Taladon met his gaze. "We didn't kidnap any children."

"We've already told you, we came to fight Malvel," added Harkman.

"Lies!" roared the villager. "I'll give you to the count of three to come clean. One..."

Taladon searched the crowd desperately for help, but Lennard was still cowering behind the cart. Then he spotted another figure. A young man with neat dark hair and a long moustache, dressed in a red cloak and leaning on a knobbly wooden staff.

"Two..."

Something about the man held Taladon's attention. He was watching them curiously, but he didn't seem angry like the other villagers. *And he's not throwing rotten vegetables at us either!*

"Three!" finished the giant. Then he lashed his whip at Taladon's back.

BEWARE THE SWAMPS

Taladon closed his eyes, bracing himself for the sting of the whip.

But instead the giant villager let out a sudden shriek. A chorus of gasps rose up all around, and Taladon opened his eyes.

"What the...?" breathed Harkman.

The big villager was staring in utter horror at the whip in his hand.

Except it wasn't a whip any more. Somehow, it had transformed into a thick green snake, coiling around his forearm. The villager shook his arm desperately, and the snake fell to the dust and slithered away.

Taladon let out a long breath. *Who did that?*

A hush fell over the crowd, as though no one knew what to do next. Then the villager with the plaited red beard flung out a finger at Taladon and Harkman. "Sorcery!" he howled. "They're evil wizards, both of them, just like Malvel!"

Taladon scanned the crowd and saw the young man in the red cloak muttering under his breath. *It's him! He was the one who cast the spell. Now it looks like he's casting another one...*

There was a clanking sound, and the metal catches of the stocks all flew open at once.

Taladon caught Harkman's eye. The

soldier nodded. "Now!"

Both of them heaved upwards at once, swinging the stocks open and pushing free. The big villager took a step forward, raising his fists to attack.

"That way!" shouted Taladon, pointing to an alleyway leading off the village square. He darted through the crowd, Harkman at his heels.

At first the villagers all seemed too stunned to move. Then one made a grab for Taladon. Taladon shoved the man aside and raced down the alleyway, with Harkman close behind, turning left, then right. The yells of the villagers sounded behind them as they gave chase.

"In here!" hissed a voice, and a

pair of hands grabbed Taladon and
Harkman, tugging them sideways,
under an arch. Taladon found himself
in a small courtyard, empty except
for a pair of horses tied up by a stack
of crates. The red-cloaked wizard
who had freed them from the stocks
pushed Taladon and Harkman into
the shadows beside a wall, then
pressed up next to them. They waited,
panting, as the crowd of villagers
surged past their hiding place.

"Who are you?" Harkman
demanded, when the noise of the
rabble had died down.

The red-cloaked stranger offered
him a hand to shake. "Kato, at your
service. I am the Wizard of Gorgonia,
and a servant of King Arun."

"You saved us," said Taladon. "Why?"

"Malvel has taken the castle," Kato explained. "He stole nearly all my power, and threw me out along with my king. If you truly mean to stop him, I am bound to help you. You must travel to the castle, but beware the swamps. They lie in your path. Something terrible lives there, something which—"

"Here they are!" screamed a voice. Whirling round, Taladon saw that some of the villagers had spotted them from the street. They were carrying weapons again – scythes and pitchforks, and even some battered old swords. Quickly, they spilled into the courtyard, surrounding

Taladon, Kato and Harkman. Taladon spotted his own sword and shield in the hands of the red-bearded villager, and Harkman's bow, gripped by a tall, gaunt man.

Kato stepped out to face the villagers. "Don't worry," he murmured to Taladon. "I'll put a protection spell on us." A green light began to glow around his fingers. Then it fizzled and died away into nothing.

"Run out of magic, have you?" jeered the big villager with the silver ponytail. He had found a spear from somewhere. "No wonder you couldn't stop Malvel!"

"Failure!" shouted another villager.

"Traitor!" added a third.

"Let's teach them a lesson they won't

forget," growled the big man.

Taladon rolled and sprang up, barging into the nearest villager and knocking him off balance. He grabbed the man's arm and prised away the rusty sword he was holding, then spun to parry a scythe that came slicing down at him.

Shouts filled the square as Harkman attacked, cracking two heads together and snatching up a fallen pitchfork. Taladon heard a deep bellow and turned to see the big villager barrelling towards him.

Taladon sidestepped at the last moment and the man flew past, straight into the stack of wooden crates. Taladon whirled his blade, knocking aside a dagger thrust by a

villager. He kicked his attacker hard
in the stomach, bringing up his sword
for a downward swipe, then stopping.
*We can't hurt them – they're only
innocent villagers!* But more were

pressing into the courtyard, blocking off all hope of escape.

Turning, Taladon saw another villager charging at him – a huge woman in a blacksmith's apron, wielding a massive iron mace. She brought the metal club whistling down, and he met the blow full on with his sword.

CLANG! Taladon's arm jolted as his rusty blade shattered, leaving him with nothing more than a shard of metal in his hand. *If only I'd had my real sword...*

But it was too late. A circle of villagers were pressing in on him, weapons levelled. Harkman was out of sight, and so was Kato. Taladon was on his own – and unarmed.

With a savage grin, the blacksmith stepped forward and raised her mace a second time.

1

THE GREEN-EYED
GIRL

There was a rush of air and the
blacksmith's eyes widened. She
ducked and an arrow flew over her
head then struck the wooden crates
with a solid *thunk*.

Another arrow whirred past, and
the villagers all dived on the ground.

Only Taladon stayed standing. On
the far side of the courtyard, he saw

that Harkman already had a third arrow nocked on his bowstring and aimed right at the blacksmith. Taladon saw that the gaunt man who had taken Harkman's bow was squirming on the ground, held firmly under the soldier's boot.

"That's enough!" growled Harkman. "Step away from the squire."

Scowling, the blacksmith laid her mace down. Taladon edged away, past the red-bearded villager. "I believe those are mine," he said, taking back his sword and shield. The villager glared, but with Harkman's arrow trained on him, he didn't protest.

Taladon felt the familiar weight of his weapons again. The sword had been forged by his brother Henry, an apprentice blacksmith. Sheathing the blade, he crossed to the horses at the side of the courtyard and untied them.

As he led the horses to Harkman, the blacksmith stepped forward again, glowering fiercely at the pair of Avantians. "You won't be able to shoot all of us," she said.

"That's true," admitted Harkman, staring right back at her. "Just the first few fools who try anything."

"I'll happily be a fool," said the woman. "For the sake of our children." Then she snatched up her mace and charged.

"Don't shoot her!" called Taladon, as he scrambled on to one of the horses.

"Of course I'm not going to shoot her!" Harkman snapped back, swinging himself on to the other horse.

Together they kicked their heels and sped out through the alleyway, just in time before the villagers came crowding after them. Taladon cast a quick glance behind and saw Kato standing still amongst the tide of villagers, one hand raised in farewell. *Good luck*, the wizard mouthed, then the horses veered round the corner, and Kato was lost from view.

They flew through the streets, hooves hammering the cobblestones. They galloped through the square and on, towards the outskirts of the village. Taladon couldn't stop thinking about the lost children, and the desperation he had seen in the villagers' eyes. *If Malvel's taken those children, we'll get them back!*

"Hey!" shouted a familiar voice from the shadows.

Taladon reined in his horse and

peered closer. Crouching down in a muddy patch of ground was a gold-armoured man, hiding behind a low wall. A pig snuffled close by, eyeing the nobleman with obvious disapproval.

"Wait for me," Sir Lennard hissed, then he clambered on top of the wall and threw himself on to the back of Taladon's horse. The poor creature let out a neigh of shock, then bolted onwards.

Together Taladon, Harkman and Sir Lennard rode out of the village.

No one said a word as they galloped over the sloping plains, heading for the black castle on the horizon. Sir Lennard's silence was welcome, but Taladon couldn't help feeling a twinge of disappointment as he watched Harkman riding just up ahead. *Just when I thought he was coming round to me!*

At last the plain began to level out, and Taladon caught his breath at the sight which greeted them. Lying in their path, at the edge of the dark jungle, were the swamps – a maze of murky grey streams and pools of water, overhung by twisted trees growing on the banks, their branches covered in creeping vines.

As they trotted closer, a mist swirled around them, and the air felt cold and dank on Taladon's skin. Something shifted in the water close by, and Taladon saw with a shudder that it was a snake coiling just beneath the surface. Abruptly both horses came to a halt, nervously swishing their tails as though they didn't dare go any further.

What was it that Kato the wizard had said? *Beware of the swamps. Something terrible lives there...*

"Keep an eye out for those missing children," said Taladon. "If there really is a monster in the swamps, perhaps it's captured them."

"If so, we're probably too late to save them," said Lennard, his voice full of his usual confidence again. "I say we find a way round."

"There isn't one," said Harkman, bluntly. "Besides, the longer we delay, the more powerful Malvel will become. We'll have to cross the swamp."

Taladon felt a cold shiver run down his spine at the thought of it, but he nodded all the same. *It's the only way.*

"We can leave the horses here," he
said.

"But...really, I don't think..."
spluttered Lennard, as they
dismounted. Then he fell into a
gloomy silence.

Taladon patted the horses' flanks and they took off, galloping away. Then the three of them set off on foot, picking their way cautiously through the swamp.

Dead trees had fallen here and there,

forming bridges across the pools. All the same, Taladon's boots were soon squelching wet. Other than the whine of mosquitoes across the surface, everything was eerily quiet. Sir Lennard took the lead, glancing back frequently to check his companions were still there. "I'll go first, in case of danger," he announced. "But we should stick together. So I can protect you."

Taladon couldn't help smiling, and he saw Harkman's mouth twitch too. The young soldier fell into step beside him, as Lennard forged on ahead. "Sorry," Harkman grunted, without looking at Taladon.

"What do you mean?" asked Taladon.

Harkman cleared his throat. "I was...er...wrong about you. Thought you wouldn't last long on a real Quest."

"I wouldn't have, without you," said Taladon, grinning. "That blacksmith would have bashed my brains out!"

Harkman smiled too. "Maybe you're right. I'm still sorry, though. I'm the youngest of five, you know. Everything I have, I had to work for. So I suppose seeing you as Prince Hugo's squire, living in the palace and all..."

"Quiet!" interrupted Lennard, suddenly.

Taladon saw that he was staring at something a short way off, half hidden by the mists. It was a small

figure, sitting on a fallen tree. A girl, no more than six years old, kicking her feet above the waters of the swamp.

The children who were stolen from the village... She must be one of them!

"Don't be afraid, child!" called Sir

Lennard, his voice quavering slightly.

The girl looked around, and Taladon drew in a sharp breath. The child's eyes were bright green, glowing softly in the gloom.

BEAST OF THE SWAMPS

The girl's face was strangely blank.
"What's wrong with her?" said
Harkman. The girl beckoned silently
to the three of them, then hoisted
herself up on to the fallen tree and set
off, skipping away across the swamp.

"After her!" roared Sir Lennard,
and he began stumbling towards the
fallen tree.

"I don't like this," muttered Harkman.

"Me neither," said Taladon. "But we can't just leave her here. It's too dangerous."

Harkman nodded, and together they followed Sir Lennard.

The girl moved fast, as though she knew every inch of the swamp. Taladon and his companions struggled to keep up. Often their boots went splashing into the water, and once Sir Lennard fell headlong into a murky pool, leaving him soaked and dripping.

All three of them were panting by the time the girl stopped in a small, round patch of land, her green eyes glowing as she waited.

The island was totally bare, without even a tree growing on it. Taladon squirmed as they arrived. *Something's not right.* "Where are you taking us?" he asked, but the girl didn't reply.

"Stay where you are, little girl," puffed Sir Lennard. "I'm coming to save you!"

"Wait!" began Harkman, but Lennard had already rushed forward, reaching out for the girl's shoulder.

Whhhhhooosh!

A fountain of spray shot up from the swamp as something massive leapt out of the water, landing in a crouch on the island like a boulder from a catapult. Taladon felt the ground shake through his boots.

Lennard flinched and stumbled. The

girl darted away, hopping across the water, her feet finding stepping stones beneath the surface, until the mists swallowed her and she was gone.

Harkman was already fumbling for an arrow. Taladon whipped his blade from its sheath and crouched down behind his shield, heart thumping.

Slowly, the swamp creature raised itself to its full height, streams of water flowing off its huge body. Sir Lennard froze, blood draining from his face. Taladon's heart beat faster, and he felt his mouth go dry.

"What in the name of Avantia...?" whispered Harkman.

It was a huge greenish-skinned monster, three times as tall as a man. His chest was rock-solid with muscle.

An ogre! The creature had four arms, as thick as the branches of an oak tree, and two giant teeth jutted up from his lower jaw. He glared at them with his tiny yellow eyes, and his hair writhed. With a lurch of his stomach,

Taladon realised it wasn't hair at all
– it was a nest of snakes, hissing and
rearing from the ogre's scalp.

"No," said Sir Lennard, his voice
hoarse. "No, no, no!"

"Do something!" yelled Harkman.
"You're the Master of the Beasts. I'd
say this is a Beast!"

But Sir Lennard just kept on
gaping. The ogre licked his lips with
a forked blue tongue, and stalked
forward with slow, thumping steps...

With lightning speed, Harkman
had sent an arrow whizzing into the
Beast's side. The ogre simply tore it
out, tossed it aside and kept walking.
Thump! Thump! Two more arrows
found their mark, but the ogre broke
the shafts with a sweep of an arm,

leaving the arrowheads buried in his flesh. He let out a savage growl and reached out with three of his hands to grab Taladon, Harkman and Lennard.

Taladon swung his sword, slicing at the ogre's fingertips. The Beast's hand recoiled. Chancing a quick look, Taladon saw Harkman dodge, but another of the ogre's fists caught him a glancing blow and he fell to one knee, clutching at his shoulder.

"Help!"

The shriek cut through the air, and Taladon saw that Sir Lennard had been too slow. The ogre held him tightly in his third fist, raising him up into the air. The Beast's stubby fingers curled around the Golden Armour, while the snakes on his head snapped

hungrily at Lennard's face.

"Let him go!" yelled Taladon, rushing forward. But the Beast kicked his shield hard, a battering blow which lifted Taladon off his feet and tossed him on to his back.

The smell of the ogre was in his nostrils now, a sickening stink of swamp water. Taladon tried to roll away, but the Beast stamped on his shoulder, crushing him into the mud.

The ogre loomed above, a four-armed bulk of shadow. He raised a fist as big as a boulder, blotting out the blood-red sun of Gorgonia. Any second now, it would come slamming down to break Taladon's skull like an egg. Then down it came, speeding faster and faster...

STORY TWO

A NEW MASTER

"Come on, Taladon! You teach that ogre a lesson!"

Tom turned at the voice. To his surprise, he saw that a small crowd had gathered in the darkened library. There were stable boys, kitchen workers, squires and maids, but it was a rosy-cheeked woman in an apron who had spoken. She blushed as Tom looked at her. "Dear me... Did I say that out loud?"

"Where did you all come from?" asked Tom.

"They heard you reading and came to listen," said Elenna, with a smile. "Don't look so shocked. You said it yourself – it's a good story!"

Tom grinned. "It's true. But you know, it's getting late. Maybe we should carry on tomorrow..."

A chorus of protests broke the hush of the library.

"Oh go on, finish it now!"

"You can't stop there!"

"We won't make a peep!"

Elenna raised an eyebrow. "Well?"

"I suppose I *could* carry on," said Tom. "After all, I can't leave my father in the clutches of a swamp ogre..."

TO THE CASTLE

CRUNCH!

Taladon drove the edge of his shield hard into the ogre's shin, and the Beast roared with pain, stepping back. The pressure on Taladon's shoulder vanished, and he rolled to one side. The next moment the Beast's fist drove down into the mud with a squelching *thud*, just where Taladon's head had been. *That was a close one!*

But as he tried to scramble upright, Taladon found that he couldn't move. Glancing over his shoulder, he saw that a corner of his tunic was caught fast under the ogre's knuckles.

Before he could react, two more of the ogre's fists came speeding at him, one from each side. With a ripping sound, Taladon tore his snagged tunic free and dived, feeling a rush of wind as the nearest fist whistled over his back. He came down head first in the mud, somersaulting into a crouch, his breath coming in rapid pants.

A bowstring thrummed. Taladon looked up to see that Harkman had loosed an arrow at the Beast. The ogre dodged, but Harkman smoothly fitted another arrow and fired it. Then

another, and another. The missiles
zipped over the Beast, slicing the heads
off the rearing snakes which were
snapping at Sir Lennard.

Taladon sent another arrow with a
thunk into the Beast's wrist, and at last
the ogre let go, dumping Sir Lennard
in the mud like a sack of potatoes.

Slipping and sliding, the nobleman rose and scurried over to Taladon, half his armour caked in pond slime. "What are you waiting for?" howled Sir Lennard. "Run for your lives!"

The Master of the Beasts raced away across a fallen tree trunk and disappeared behind a clump of trees.

The ogre snapped off the arrow embedded in his wrist. Then he turned on Taladon and Harkman, his teeth gleaming in the half-light.

"For once," said Taladon, "I think Sir Lennard might have a point."

He and Harkman turned and fled. They dashed across the fallen trunk and behind the clump of trees, splattering swamp water with every step. Taladon sped up, overtaking Sir

Lennard and charging through the mists of the swamp.

A roar rose behind them, swaying the dead branches of the trees. The ground shook with heavy footsteps as the ogre gave chase. Taladon cast a glance behind them, but he couldn't see the Beast through the mist.

He's getting closer, though. Taladon could hear the ogre's snorting breaths now, and smell his foul odour. *We can't outrun him...which means we'll have to hide.*

Glancing to his left, Taladon spotted a thick clump of bushes. "Follow me!" he called, veering to the side. He dived behind the bushes, followed by Harkman and Sir Lennard. They all crouched down low, holding their breath and listening.

Thump! Thump! Thump!

The footsteps of the Beast carried on, thundering past their hiding place, until at last they faded into the eerie silence of the swamp.

"I've never seen anything like that... *thing*," whispered Sir Lennard.

Harkman snorted. "Doesn't your father have a painting of it?"

"Come on," said Taladon. "Let's get out of here."

The trees became thicker as they set off again through the swamp, treading carefully. Soon they were picking their way through the thick, shadowy jungle beyond. They travelled in silence, and Taladon knew they were all thinking of the monstrous ogre, and the strange green-eyed girl.

She led us to the Beast on purpose. But why? Is it Malvel's doing?

At last the trees thinned out and they emerged on to a flat, grassy plain. Up ahead, the familiar black fortress stood stark against the red sky.

The Castle of Gorgonia!

"How do we get inside?" said Harkman, squinting up at the castle walls. "The drawbridge is shut. And Malvel isn't just going to invite us in."

"Maybe there's another way..." said Taladon.

But before he could finish, a blood-curdling howl echoed through the jungle behind them.

Whirling around, Taladon saw a giant figure come crashing through the dark undergrowth, four arms flailing with fury. It was the ogre, head lowered, grunting and growling as he bore down on them.

"To the castle!" yelled Harkman. They took off across the plain, but before long Sir Lennard was lagging behind, struggling to keep up.

Glancing back, Taladon saw that the ogre had broken free of the trees and was stomping towards them, gaining ground all the time.

"I thought the golden leg armour was supposed to give you magical speed!" Harkman snapped, but Sir Lennard looked too scared to reply.

As they reached the castle, Taladon skidded to a halt. The black walls were surrounded by a wide moat.

No way across. He turned, just as the
others arrived next to him. The ogre
was closer than ever, and Taladon
could have sworn its lips were curled
into a horrible smile of triumph.

*A moat behind us, and an ogre in
front... We're trapped!*

MALVEL'S PRISONERS

"There! In the water!"

Harkman was pointing. Taladon scanned the surface of the moat. Then his heart leapt as he saw something. A small iron grate was built into the black stone of the wall, rising just above the waterline.

A drainage channel! Could that be our way into the castle? There was only one way to find out. "Everyone into the moat!" yelled Taladon.

"Are you sure?" mumbled Lennard. Then he yelped as Harkman shoved him hard, sending him toppling down into the water with a huge splash.

Taladon took one last look at the ogre, then he and Harkman dived after Sir Lennard.

The water swallowed up Taladon in a sudden rush of silence, then he surfaced, spluttering. He swam towards the grate. His fingers closed over the metal edges, but it was stuck fast, and even when he strained his muscles it wouldn't budge an inch.

"The Golden Armour!" he shouted. "Sir Lennard, use its magical strength to get this open!" But as he looked back, he saw that the nobleman was floundering, barely able to keep afloat as the armour weighed him down.

Harkman seized hold of one side of the grate, and together he and Taladon tugged at it, finally wrenching it away from the wall with a squeal of metal.

"I'm drowning!" cried Sir Lennard. Taladon and Harkman grabbed hold of the nobleman and shoved him through into the drainage channel.

A huge splash sounded behind them. Looking back, Taladon saw that the ogre had plunged into the moat and was wading towards them, clawing at the water with his four powerful hands...

Harkman scrambled into the half-submerged tunnel and Taladon followed him in. "Watch out!" cried Harkman, grabbing Taladon by the

arms and tugging him in further, just as two of the ogre's grasping arms came snatching for his heels. Taladon felt the Beast's fingers brush his boot, but he yanked his leg clear as he tumbled into the tunnel.

The ogre howled with fury. He battered the inside walls of the tunnel with his fists. But there was no way his body could fit through. *We made it...* The three of them crouched in the dank drainage channel, sodden and panting as they gradually caught their breath.

"Well then," grunted Harkman, at last. "Time to capture this castle."

The drainage channel smelled terrible, and the stench got even worse as they crawled further along it. Taladon soon found out why. The tunnel curved upwards, and then he was heaving himself up and out through a privy on the ground floor of the castle. Dripping with foul water, he reached back in to help Harkman up. Then both of them dragged Sir Lennard out.

The nobleman collapsed on the floor, soaking wet, his blond moustache drooping. "The horror…" he murmured, looking utterly miserable.

Harkman glowered down at him. "That Golden Armour is supposed to give you magical strength, and magical speed, and magical *bravery* too! So why isn't it working?"

Sir Lennard hung his head, refusing to meet the soldier's eyes. "I don't know," he said in a small voice. "Perhaps it's because there hasn't been a Master of the Beasts in so long, but... well, the truth is it's *never* worked. I thought if I wore it long enough, some of its magic might rub off on me, but... well...I don't really understand."

"I do," said Harkman, through gritted teeth. "The armour doesn't work because you're not worthy to wear it!"

Sir Lennard sniffed, and Taladon felt a flicker of sympathy for the nobleman. "Don't worry," said Taladon. "I'm sure it'll work in time. Let's keep our minds on the Quest. Malvel's got to be here somewhere – so let's find him!"

Taladon drew his sword and Harkman fitted an arrow to his bow, as Sir Lennard clambered to his feet. Then they set off, stepping through the doorway of the privy and into a stone corridor.

None of the torches were lit, and shadows clung to every corner. The only sound was their footsteps as they crept across the flagstones.

The castle seems totally deserted...

Taladon led them through an empty banqueting hall and down a winding spiral staircase. As they descended, a spider scuttled away from his foot, and Taladon felt a chill creep down his spine. *Something's not right here...* But he had a strange feeling that this was the way to Malvel – down, deeper into the castle.

At the bottom of the steps they found themselves in a hallway with a barred door at the end of it. There was no light, except for a soft green glow coming from within the prison cell. When Taladon saw where it came from, he stopped dead in his tracks, his heart racing.

"It can't be..." breathed Sir Lennard, in shock.

The cell was crowded with prisoners – children dressed in rags, most of them surely no more than five years old. They stood utterly still, as though they were sleepwalking. And every single one of them had eyes that glowed bright green.

"The children from the village," said Harkman.

"We must rescue them at once," said Sir Lennard.

He stepped forward, but Taladon held him back with one arm. "I'm not sure about that," said Taladon. "Remember that girl in the swamps? She led us into danger. I think Malvel's put a spell on them."

"Do you, indeed?" said a taunting voice from the steps behind them. A young man came down into the hallway, smiling. He wore a dark green hooded cloak, and his eyes shone with triumph.

Malvel!

The Dark Wizard raised his hand and the cell door flew open with a bang. The children spilled out, twenty or thirty of them, scurrying like rats to surround Taladon and his companions. The children reached for their belts and brought out sharp daggers, glinting green in the light from their eyes. Then, slowly, they levelled their blades at the three Avantians.

THE GREEN JEWEL

"What have you done to them?" shouted Taladon, as he backed up against Harkman and Sir Lennard, all of them drawing their weapons.

"Just a little spell to make them my servants," replied Malvel. "They do what I wish, and whatever they see, I see too." He shook his head, and laughed. "You heroes are so delightfully predictable! Kidnap a few children, and you'll do absolutely anything to save them. It's a terrible weakness."

"Fond of his own voice, isn't he?" muttered Harkman.

"Like in the swamps," said Malvel, ignoring the soldier. "I did so enjoy watching dear Sasha lead you right into the clutches of Magror the Swamp Ogre! I think she enjoyed it too, to be honest. Step forward, Sasha, don't be shy."

A girl took a step out from among the circle – the girl they had seen back in the swamp. Her eyes looked just as green and empty as those of the other children.

"I'm only sorry that the ogre didn't finish you off nice and quickly," said

Malvel, with a sigh. "But you needn't worry. I can always rely on my little servants."

The children all took one step inwards, the circle closing in on Taladon, Harkman and Lennard.

I've got to play for time...

"Are you such a coward that you won't face us yourself?" asked Taladon.

Malvel's gaze fell on him, and the Dark Wizard's brow creased. "Ah yes...Taladon, squire to the foolish young Hugo. You could have stayed out of this so easily, you know. Well, it's too late now."

Malvel clasped an object at his throat, and Taladon saw something glinting between his fingers. A pendant hung from a cord around the Dark Wizard's neck, with a glowing green jewel set in it. *Exactly the same green as the children's eyes. So that's how he's controlling them!*

"Kill them!" cried Malvel. The children surged forward, daggers raised to strike.

"We can't fight children!" shouted Harkman.

Taladon turned to Sir Lennard, grabbing the nobleman by the shoulders and pushing him down into a crouch. Then he set his boot on Lennard's shoulder.

"What are you doing?" yelped Sir Lennard.

"Just trust me!" Taladon shot back.

As the children rushed towards

them, Taladon leapt up, using Sir
Lennard as a springboard. He sailed
through the air, pulling up his legs
and jumping over the charging
children. Then he bent his knees,
cushioning his landing on the
flagstones beyond.

Malvel threw out his hand, pointing at Taladon and muttering a spell under his breath. But Taladon lunged and grabbed hold of the pendant dangling from the wizard's neck.

"How dare you?" screeched Malvel, but Taladon tore the pendant away, snapping its cord. The pendant fell with a *clink* on the stone flagstones. Then the light of the green jewel winked out, leaving it dark and dull.

At the same instant a flash of green lit up the hall, and the children came stumbling to a halt, blinking and lowering their daggers. They looked dazed, as if they had no idea where they were. Then Taladon felt a surge of relief as he saw that their eyes were slowly turning back to normal.

"It's over, Malvel," said Taladon.

"Never!" howled the Dark Wizard. "I can still destroy you!" He twisted free and darted across the hallway, but Harkman was quicker. The soldier dived, slamming into Malvel and pinning him to the wall.

"You're going nowhere," said Harkman, firmly.

Together, the three Avantians dragged Malvel into the prison cell and fixed manacles around his wrists.

"Thanks for the help back there," Taladon said to Sir Lennard.

"Don't mention it," said the nobleman, brightening. Then he looked away. "I mean, I suppose... It was all your doing, really."

Taladon smiled.

"Excuse me, sir?"

Turning, Taladon saw Sasha standing before the group of children. They had all gathered in the doorway to the cell, looking lost and confused. "We were just wondering..." said Sasha. "Where are we?"

"It's a long story," Harkman told her. He finished attaching the chains to Malvel and straightened up. "We'll get you back to your village, don't you worry. Then we'll be off back home to—"

The dungeon shuddered with a deep, rumbling sound, cutting Harkman off. Everyone looked around nervously. *What is that?* The rumble came again, closer this time, and the cell floor seemed to shake.

A low chuckle echoed through the cell, and Taladon looked down to see Malvel grinning up at them, his eyes glittering with malice. "Did you think your Quest was over?" the Dark Wizard taunted. "I'm afraid not...the swamp ogre is coming for you now. You've angered him, and you will pay the price. You and these precious children!"

"What does he mean?" stammered Sir Lennard.

But before anyone could reply, the cell wall exploded with a deafening crash and a shower of stone.

Taladon coughed and spluttered as a gigantic figure stepped through the cloud of brick dust, fists bunched like rocks, chest heaving.

Magror...

"Get the children out!" Taladon

told his companions. "I'll distract the Beast..."

But it was too late. The swamp ogre's tiny, gleaming eyes locked on to Sasha and the crowd of village children cowering in the doorway to the cell. The Beast took a step forward, sniffed the air and licked his lips, his teeth glinting with saliva.

"Oh, didn't I mention?" said Malvel. "Magror loves children. He thinks they're just *delicious*."

THE LAST CHILD

Taladon drew his sword and stepped into the path of the Beast. "Leave the children out of this," he said.

Magror shambled to a halt, glaring at him. Then with a snort the ogre lunged forward, a giant fist pummelling in from the left.

Taladon ducked low, dodging the punch. He swung his sword, slicing deep into the ogre's ankle, then rolled

between Magror's legs, springing up into a crouch beyond. *All those hours of training have paid off.*

The Beast let out a fearsome roar and whirled around. Through Magror's sturdy legs, Taladon saw

Harkman drag Malvel to his feet, sword at his back, as Sir Lennard herded the children out through the gaping hole in the cell wall. Harkman nodded at Taladon, before pushing Malvel over the rubble, following Lennard and the children into the darkness.

Taladon stared up at the towering form of the Beast.

Then Magror's fists clenched again, and Taladon darted out through the open prison door, across the hall and up the curving spiral staircase. *I've got to lead him away from the children!*

The whole castle seemed to quake as the ogre followed, stomping across the flagstones. Taladon's heart beat faster as he heard the ogre behind him, taking the steps several at a time. Glancing over his shoulder, he saw the Beast's bulk squeezing round the stairwell, his bulging muscles scraping at the walls. Then Magror raised all four fists at once, and brought them slamming down on one of the steps.

Taladon stumbled as the staircase juddered, and a crack spread up from where the Beast had struck. The stone broke beneath Taladon's feet. He pushed his legs harder, racing up the steps, but with a deafening crash the stairs fell away beneath him. Taladon's body lurched downwards and he grasped desperately, fingers finding a step further up and clinging on.

The whole weight of Taladon's body

swayed, dangling in mid-air. A quick glance below, and he saw the curve of the steps further down. *Too far.* If he let go, he'd break his legs on impact – maybe even crack his skull.

Drawing on his last ounce of strength, Taladon hauled himself up, scrambling on to the cracked stairway above. His muscles burned as he staggered on up the steps. But a deafening roar echoed all around, and he looked back to see Magror launch himself up over the missing steps with incredible strength, landing with a thunderous impact not far behind.

Once again the ogre swung all four fists, driving them like battering rams into the wall. The ceiling caved in, chunks of rock raining down. Taladon flung his shield over his head, stone debris crashing against it, the shock throbbing through his arm.

He leapt up the last few steps and veered right, charging down a corridor. He could feel the ground shake as Magror pursued him. Up ahead, suits of armour stood guard along the walls, and Taladon tugged each one over as he ran, sending them crashing to the floor. Looking back, he saw Magror ploughing onwards, scattering the pieces of metal like leaves.

I can't just keep running... I've got to fight back!

Taladon snatched a halberd from a bracket on the wall and hurled it back down the corridor. But Magror simply grunted and caught the weapon. Then he flung it back, sending it speeding towards Taladon...

Taladon threw himself to the side, and the halberd buried itself with a *thud* in an oak door at the end of the corridor, the long handle quivering.

Taladon raced for the door. He barely had the energy left to run, but if he didn't, the ogre would crush him with those giant fists.

The Beast began to roar, a savage, wailing battle cry, just as Taladon reached the door. He flung it open and dived through, rolling on to grass. A moment later, he heard the stone doorway explode as the ogre burst through.

Springing to his feet, Taladon saw that he was in a courtyard under the open red sky of Gorgonia. Ahead was the drawbridge, still chained shut. *I've got to face the Beast!* Taladon turned and took up a fighting crouch with his sword and shield raised.

Magror paced towards him, the

sun gleaming on his green skin.
Then the Beast stopped dead and
sniffed. Slowly his head turned, and
his gaze fell on a horseless cart at
the side of the courtyard. He strode
towards it, reaching it in three steps.
He gripped the cart with all four
fists and flipped it upside down. The

cart landed with a crash. Its timbers shuddered, and something fell, rolling out of it. Taladon caught his breath. It was a little boy, dressed in a ragged tunic, his huge eyes wild with fear. He cowered in a ball, trembling and staring up at the ogre.

He must be one of the children
Malvel captured...

"Run!" yelled Taladon. "Get out of here!" But the boy seemed rooted to the spot.

Magror gave a soft grunt, then slowly he reached out one hand for the child, strings of drool dangling from his teeth.

5

THE ARMOUR'S CHOICE

Taladon raced over the flagstones.
His muscles burned with exhaustion,
but he ignored the pain and pushed
harder. *I've got to save that child, if
it's the last thing I do...*

He flung himself forwards, diving
headfirst. With a soft *thump* he
shoved the boy aside so that he went
rolling out of harm's way.

Lying on the ground, panting, Taladon turned upwards just as the Beast's fist closed around his torso and lifted him up into the air. Taladon struggled, but the grip was unyielding. Magror raised Taladon to his face, so close that Taladon could see his own squirming reflection in the pebble-like eyes of the Beast. He swung his sword, but the ogre held him just out of reach and he cut nothing but air. He felt as though he were being held in an iron vice.

"Taladon!"

The shout came from the far side of the courtyard. Glancing over the Beast's shoulder, Taladon saw that Harkman had emerged into the courtyard from another doorway, followed by Lennard with the chained-up Malvel and the crowd of village children.

Harkman was busy with his bow, setting an arrow on the string as the frightened boy from the cart scurried to join his friends.

"No!" Taladon shouted, choking out the word. "The drawbridge... Save yourselves!"

It's too late for me. Taladon knew it, deep in his bones. He could feel the ogre's fingers squeezing tighter and tighter, crushing the air from his lungs.

At least I died to save the boy's life.

The ogre grinned horribly, opening his jaws wide like a gaping cavern. Taladon's body throbbed with pain, every muscle screaming in agony as the life was squeezed out of him. Any moment now, his ribcage would shatter like an eggshell.

Then something ran through him – a strange wave of cold – and all at once the pain was gone. His clothes seemed to have become heavier and firmer.

The ogre's piggy eyes narrowed in confusion, and he growled. His three other hands flew to Taladon's chest, pushing in to crush his enemy. But Taladon didn't feel a thing. *What in all Avantia...?* Then he looked down, and couldn't believe his eyes.

The Golden Armour!

Somehow, he was wearing it now instead of Lennard. The glittering golden plates covered every inch of

his body, firmly resisting the grip of
the Beast. *The breastplate, the leg
armour...the gauntlets and the boots!*
Then he realised he was wearing the
helmet too. He looked up and saw Sir
Lennard, eyes wide with shock, now
dressed only in his tunic, breeches

and boots. The nobleman patted himself down, but there was no doubt that the armour was gone from his body.

A warm surge of courage rose up in Taladon's chest. *The courage of the golden chainmail!* Taladon had heard so many stories about the Golden Armour. The strength of the breastplate, the speed and endurance of the golden leg armour, the mastery of the sword given by the gauntlets, and the jumping power of the golden boots... *Magror doesn't stand a chance now!*

Taladon brought the hilt of his sword slamming down on to Magror's fists, hammering at them again and again. The ogre flinched, loosening

his grip, and Taladon squirmed
free, dropping to the flagstones and
landing in a crouch. The Beast tried
to catch him again, but Taladon
dodged and launched a flying kick
at Magror's bloated stomach. It
connected with stunning force, and
the Beast stumbled backwards across
the courtyard.

A gasp rose up from among
the village children as Taladon
straightened, gaze locked on the
swamp ogre.

"The Armour has chosen him,"
said Harkman, his voice hoarse with
wonder. "I can't believe it... Taladon is
the true Master of the Beasts!"

6

THE GOOD AVANTIANS

Magror let out an anguished howl of fury, so loud the children shrank back in terror. Then he barrelled towards Taladon, four hands clenched into fists, shaking the courtyard with every step.

Taladon stood his ground, waiting calmly. *I'm not afraid of you, Magror!*

At the last moment Taladon ducked

low and felt a fist go whistling above his head. Then he attacked, swinging his blade in wide, flashing arcs, with the magic of the gauntlets thrumming through his hands. Magror jerked away from the sword and unleashed two more savage punches, but Taladon dodged the first and deflected the second with his shield. *Whack!*

His whole arm rang with the vibrations of the blow, but there was no time to think about the pain. Magror was roaring now, shaking with anger. He swung wildly with his fists, missing Taladon and smashing a chunk out of a flagstone. Taladon ducked and weaved, dancing on his feet just out of reach of the ogre's

deadly blows. "Harkman!" he yelled.
"Lower the drawbridge!"

Out of the corner of his eye he
saw the soldier running across the
courtyard. A moment later there
was a low, creaking sound and the
drawbridge swung down, metal

chains rasping until the wood
clunked into place over the moat.

Magror shook his snake-hair with
rage as he saw the village children
streaming across the drawbridge
to safety, followed by Lennard.
Harkman shoved Malvel after them,
pausing just before the archway to
give Taladon a final grim nod. Then he
was gone too.

The swamp ogre turned away from
Taladon and stomped towards the
drawbridge. Quickly Taladon drew
on the speed of the golden leg armour
and darted to overtake, his feet
moving faster than he could believe.
He skidded to a halt in the middle of
the bridge, just as Magror shambled
out beneath the archway.

"No way past, Magror," Taladon said.

The Beast's terrible gaze fell on one of the drawbridge chains. With a grunt he snatched hold of it and tugged, snapping a link at the far end of the bridge, then one at the near end so that the chain came free.

A chill ran through Taladon's blood. *He's made himself a metal whip!* And the next moment the ogre was raising his fist, the end of the chain trailing on the ground behind him, ready to swing over and smash down on to Taladon's head...

Taladon took a deep breath and drew on the speed of the leg armour. Then he lunged forward, sliding low between the ogre's massive legs. He drove his sword down hard through the final link of the chain into the drawbridge, trapping the chain in place. He held it firm with all the strength of the golden breastplate.

As the ogre swung, the chain flew taut and Magror's hand jerked backwards. Caught off balance, the Beast slipped and fell, making the timbers shudder as he landed hard on his back.

No time to lose...

Taladon pulled his sword free and leapt up on to the writhing Beast's chest, slicing and hacking at the ogre's hair until every snake hung limp and dead. Then he crouched, snatched hold of Magror's ragged collar and pushed his sword up hard under the Beast's chin.

"Give up, Magror!" he shouted.

The ogre glowered at him with utter hatred in his yellow eyes. For a moment neither of them moved. Then Magror sank back with a sigh.

Taladon felt the ogre's chest shifting and falling away beneath him, and

he saw that the Beast's whole body
was melting, transforming into grey-
green, swampy water that cascaded
off the drawbridge into the moat.
Taladon fell, his knees smacking into
the damp wood beneath. At last, all
the water was gone, and there was no

sound left except for Taladon's own heavy, panting breaths.

"I don't understand," said Sir Lennard's trembling voice from nearby. "What happened?"

Somehow, Taladon knew the answer.

He's gone back to his home in the swamps. We defeated him.

It was really over.

Taladon couldn't stop grinning as he watched the children rush into the arms of their parents.

He stood with Harkman and Sir Lennard in the village square again, but this time, instead of throwing mouldy tomatoes at them, the villagers were crowding round to thank them for saving their children.

"It was nothing," mumbled Sir Lennard, blushing.

"After everything we did to you," said the burly blacksmith, her

daughter clinging to her back. "You risked your lives for our sons and daughters." She shook Taladon's hand so hard he thought she might crush it, even through the golden gauntlet.

"Sorry about all that rotten fruit," added another villager, her arm around a little boy. "I suppose this proves Avantians aren't so bad."

"Not all of them, anyway," muttered her husband.

"Here he comes," said Harkman, laying a hand on Taladon's arm.

Turning, Taladon saw the Wizard Kato pushing through the crowd, still wearing his red robes.

"Is it done?" asked Harkman.

Kato nodded. "Thanks to you, my powers are returned, and Malvel is now safely locked away in the castle dungeon, where he belongs." The wizard looked pale though, his brow knitted with worry.

"Are you all right?" asked Taladon.

"Oh yes," said Kato, briskly. "It's just...he threatened me. He said that one day he would take his revenge. But it's quite safe. I've used magical defences to keep him in place. He won't get away easily, I promise you."

Taladon and Harkman exchanged a glance. "Just be careful," said Harkman. "There's no wizard more dangerous in all the kingdoms."

"Now, my Avantians," said the villager with the plaited red beard, throwing an arm around Taladon's shoulders. "We must repay you as best we can. A feast in your honour! You'll drink our finest local ale, and dine on roast venison."

"You're too kind," said Taladon, with a smile. "But now our Quest is complete, we must return to our king. Harkman, do you have the horn?"

Harkman drew out Aduro's glittering golden horn. "Ready?" he asked.

"Ready," said Sir Lennard.

"Goodbye," said Taladon to the villagers. "Perhaps we'll meet again one day. I certainly hope so – and as friends, next time!"

The villagers smiled and waved, as Harkman lifted the horn to his lips and blew.

7

A HERO'S HEART

"How can I ever thank you enough?"
There were tears in old King
Arun's eyes as he clasped Taladon's
gauntleted hands with gratitude.

"No need, Your Majesty," replied
Taladon. "It is an honour to serve you."

Applause rang out all around the
hall as Taladon knelt with Harkman
and Sir Lennard before the throne.
King Theo stood there, beaming as he

clapped, with the whole royal family at his side – Queen Rosalind, Prince Angelo and Prince Hugo. Aduro the wizard, too. He caught Taladon's eye with his steely gaze, and Taladon looked down, feeling embarrassed.

When King Arun had finished thanking Harkman and Sir Lennard too, he turned to King Theo. "Gorgonia will not forget what you have done for us," he vowed.

The courtiers of Avantia bowed low as King Arun crossed to Aduro's portal, the bright white shimmering tunnel through which Taladon and his companions had arrived. Then with a final wave to King Theo, the Gorgonian stepped through, and the portal closed up in a flash of light.

"Taladon," said King Theo. "Master of the Beasts."

A hush fell, and Taladon felt everyone's gaze on him. He rose to his feet, standing up taller than ever in the glittering Golden Armour.

"You have proved yourself, young man," said King Theo. "It is clear that our kingdom is in safe hands with you to protect us. And from all my son Hugo has told me, you are indeed most worthy to wear the Golden Armour. It has chosen wisely!"

Prince Hugo smiled at Taladon, and Taladon smiled back. "Thank you, Your Highness," he murmured.

"You will wait on me tomorrow, Master of the Beasts," said King Theo. "We have much to discuss."

Trumpets sounded as the king turned and left the throne room, followed by his family. The noblemen of Avantia bowed low, then a gentle hum of conversation filled the room as they began to talk amongst themselves.

"He's absolutely right, you know," said a familiar voice. Taladon turned to see Sir Lennard looking sheepish. "You're no ordinary squire. After what you did in Gorgonia... Well, you deserve the Golden Armour. I've no doubt you'll be a fine Master of the Beasts."

Taladon bowed to Sir Lennard. "And you're a fine swordsman."

Sir Lennard snorted. "Thank you... but I believe I'll stick to tournaments from now on. Much more civilised. And not a swamp ogre in sight."

Harkman stepped forward, grinning. Then he pulled Taladon in and embraced him so firmly that for a moment he could hardly breathe.

"Who would have thought it?" said Harkman, when he finally let go and took a step back. "A farm boy has

become Master of the Beasts!" He shook his head. "I'm sorry I doubted you, Taladon. It was only jealousy. But that's all in the past. From now on, whatever you need, I'm ready to help."

Taladon felt his cheeks flush. He didn't know what to say. Then Harkman glanced over Taladon's shoulder and nodded. "You'd better go, my friend. I believe there's someone who wants to talk to you."

Turning, Taladon saw the robed Aduro beckoning him to a doorway at the side of the throne room. With a parting smile at Harkman, he crossed to the wizard, his heart racing.

"So," said Aduro, one eyebrow raised. "Do you think you are ready?"

Taladon wasn't sure. Everything

seemed to be changing so fast. *What will my brother say when he hears about this? He won't be able to believe it!* All the same, he nodded. "I'm ready."

Aduro gazed deep into his eyes, then smiled. "Yes," he said. "I believe you are." He led the way out of the throne room, through the doorway and into a narrow corridor which Taladon had never seen before. "This is the way to the library," said Aduro. "There is much for you to learn there about the Beasts of Avantia."

"Wait," said Taladon.

Aduro paused, his hand resting on the handle of an ornately carved oak door at the end of the corridor.

"There must be a dozen better

warriors than me in the court," said Taladon. "I've never ridden in a tournament, or even won a duel. So why did the armour pick me?"

Aduro's eyes sparkled. "What you say is true," he said softly. "But a hero is not measured by their skill with weapons, or by how many foes they have vanquished. They are measured by the strength of their heart. Honour and courage run in your veins, Taladon. They will run in the veins of your children, and of their children too."

At last the wizard turned the handle and flung open the door. "Now come with me, Taladon. Or should I say...Master of the Beasts!"

Tom closed the ancient pages slowly, and looked up from the book. One of the young stable-hands was snoring softly, leaning back against a wall. But the rest of the people in the room were watching him, mouths agape and eyes glowing in the flickering candlelight.

"What a story!" said a laundry maid. "Is it true?"

Tom nodded. "I've never known the *Chronicles of Avantia* to lie."

The stable-hand woke with a jolt. "Get him, Taladon!" he exclaimed, then looked around with a frown. "Oh! Did I miss the end?"

"I'm afraid so," said Elenna.

"I hope that coward Lennard got what he deserved," said the boy.

"He wasn't so bad, actually," said a cook. He rubbed his eyes. "I'd better get to bed. Got to be up at dawn to bake the bread!"

The rest of the listeners, still muttering about the incredible story, slowly climbed to their feet and shuffled out of the room as well. Soon only Tom and Elenna were left.

Tom slipped the book back on to the shelf, eyeing the other volumes. "So many tales," he muttered.

"Why do you look sad?" Elenna asked.

"My father never got to tell me about all of his adventures as Master of the Beasts," Tom said.

Elenna put a hand on his shoulder. "Well, this is the next best thing," she said. After a pause, she added, "Aduro was right, you know."

"About what?"

"When he said that honour and courage would run in the veins of Taladon's children," said Elenna.

Tom blushed. "Come on, let's get some sleep. Reading about all that action has made *me* tired!" He blew out the candle, and he and Elenna climbed the stone steps from the library. When they reached the top, starlight filled the quiet palace courtyard.

Tom heard Storm whickering from the stables. As he walked to his chamber, a figure stepped out from behind a corner. Tom jumped, but then relaxed when he saw it was only Captain Harkman on patrol.

"You're up early!" he exclaimed.

"We've been in the library," said Elenna.

Harkman grunted. "Read anything interesting?"

Tom grinned, trying to imagine the grizzled man in front of him as a young soldier. "You could say that, I suppose..."

THE END

CONGRATULATIONS,
YOU HAVE COMPLETED THIS QUEST!

At the end of each chapter you were awarded a special gold coin.
The QUEST in this book was worth an amazing 14 coins.

Look at the Beast Quest totem picture inside the back cover of this book to see how far you've come in your journey to become

MASTER OF THE BEASTS.

The more books you read, the more coins you will collect!

Do you want your own
Beast Quest Totem?
1. Cut out and collect the coin below
2. Go to the Beast Quest website
3. Download and print out your totem
4. Add your coin to the totem
www.beastquest.co.uk/totem

Look out for the next series of Beast Quest! Read on for a sneak peek at ZULOK THE WINGED SPIRIT...

CHAPTER ONE

NOISES IN THE NIGHT

Tom jolted upright in bed, his heart pounding against his ribcage as he stared into the darkness. Black shapes lurked in the shadows, hunched like crouching Beasts.

As Tom's eyes adjusted, the menacing forms became nothing but a chair draped with clothes, his nightstand, the brass fireguard. His pulse began to slow.

But what woke me?

Tom shivered and reached for the sweaty blankets tangled about his legs – then froze. A piercing cry filled the night. He leapt from his bed. *Someone's in trouble!* Tom grabbed his sword and dashed from the room. Then he heard the cry again, from somewhere above.

Read ZULOK THE WINGED SPIRIT to find out more!

Fight the Beasts,
Fear the Magic

Do you want to know more
about BEAST QUEST?
Then join our Quest Club!

Visit
www.beastquest.co.uk/club
and sign up today!

Are you a collector of the Beast Quest Cards?
Visit the website for further information.